# Sebastian's Secret
# Excuses
## to Avoid Cleaning
# His Room

# Sebastian's Secret
# Excuses
## to Avoid Cleaning
# His Room

(DO NOT LET ADULTS READ THIS BOOK!!!)

**C.M. BOVE**

iUniverse, Inc.
Bloomington

Sebastian's Secret Excuses to Avoid Cleaning His Room
(Do Not Let Adults Read This Book!!!)

iUniverse books may be ordered through booksellers or by contacting:

iUniverse
1663 Liberty Drive
Bloomington, IN 47403
www.iuniverse.com
1-800-Authors (1-800-288-4677)

ISBN: 978-1-4697-7925-6 (sc)
ISBN: 978-1-4697-7926-3 (ebk)

Printed in the United States of America

iUniverse rev. date: 02/15/2012

*Why?*

## You can't make me.

It's *not* my day.

Richie is not cleaning *his* room.

I'm tired.

I feel sick.

# My leg hurts.

# I have a headache.

I'm hungry. I'm too weak. I need to eat!

It's bedtime.

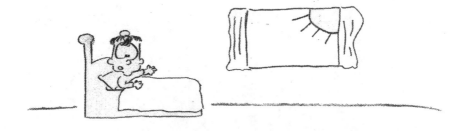

It's not my room.

There's a bug in the room.

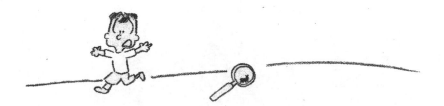

It's not fair.

In three more minutes.

It's not messy. I don't need to clean it.

You make me mad.

My friends don't have to clean *their* rooms.

This is the worst day ever!

I already cleaned it.

*You* didn't clean *your* room.

# You don't love me.

# You're mean.

# I miss Grandpa.

# Mom, I want to give you a kiss.

I forgot.

You never told me.

# Let me pet Annie first.

# I want a break.

I promise to clean later. My cousins are here.

I did not make the mess; my cousins did it.

Grandpa says I have to play outside!

I'm playing with Brandon.

# I have a sunburn.

## I'm itchy.

# I'm bleeding.

I'm sleeping. *Zzzzzzzzzzzzz . . .*

I had a bad dream.

# Mommy said I don't have to clean.

# Mom needs to help me.

I can't stop in the middle of my game.

I have to use the bathroom.

# What do you mean my room is a mess?

# This is how I like it.

# If I put things away, how will I find them?

# You didn't tell me I *had* to do it.

# You do it so much better than me.

# NO!